T0096207

Praise for *Cell #77*

"We see them in vivid glimpses: A schoolteacher deafened by the gun-butt of militarized police, husbands and uncles disappearing into unmarked cars, women giving birth in shackles, infants' first days in prisons where 'the heavy smell of orphanhood slunk over the cell's walls.' Aslan Demir's debut story collection reflects our time of ordinary people fleeing oppression, unjust wars and unnatural weather. *Cell #77* bears witness to families risking death to cross water and other borders to seek safety: 'No one would put his child in a boat unless the water was safer than the land.' Demir's lyrical fiction is led by a poetic eye that counts a woman's coma by sunsets and watches small town's shepherds 'working off their winter rust.' In answer to terror, Demir remains rooted in his Sufi training, keeping a vision that is wise and kind even in anger and grief: Knowing that 'even water hurts if it flows through a wound,' he 'keeps his faith under his left rib' and looks to the children drawing blue skies."

—**Gillian Parrish, author of** *supermoon*

"As a student, I watched Aslan's writing evolve with awe at its power and lyrical beauty. As a journalist, I marvel at his success in wooing readers to difficult stories of tyranny and genocide through gorgeous language and portraits of its victims that are as nuanced and luminous as jewels in a dirty box."

—**Gina Keating, author of** *Netflixed: The Epic Battle for America's Eyeballs*

Cell #77

Aslan Demir

BLUE DOME

Published by Blue Dome Press

335 Clifton Ave., Clifton,

NJ, 07011, USA

www.bluedomepress.com

Hardcover 978-1-68206-527-3   Epub 978-1-68206-528-0

Library of Congress Cataloging-in-Publication Data

Names: Demir, Aslan, author. | Erdoğan, Selman, illustrator.
Title: Cell #77 / Aslan Demir ; [illustrated by Selman Erdoğan].
Other titles: Cell number seventy-seven
Description: Clifton, NJ : Blue Dome Press, 2020.
Identifiers: LCCN 2019055500 (print) | LCCN 2019055501 (ebook) | ISBN 9781682065273 (hardcover) | ISBN 9781682065280 (ebook)
Subjects: LCSH: Demir, Aslan, | Women political prisoners--Turkey--Biography. | Political prisoners--Turkey--Biography. | Women journalists--Turkey--Biography. | Kurds--Civil rights--Turkey.
Classification: LCC HV9776.7 .D45 2020 (print) | LCC HV9776.7 (ebook) | DDC 818/.603 [B]--dc23
LC record available at https://lccn.loc.gov/2019055500
LC ebook record available at https://lccn.loc.gov/2019055501

Cover design: Sinan Özdemir

With gratitude to Prof. Gillian Parrish
and Lindenwood University MFA Writers

Contents

1

#77

If I kiss your tears to enshrine

Will your innocence pass on to me?

It is 3 a.m. Here they go again: prisoner number 3, 8, and 13. At the same time every night they start crying, not letting me sleep. Joined by other convicts, sometimes they make an annoying—yet musical and heartbreaking—noise. I know it's 13 who starts the siren. He is so loud. Nobody knows what the problem is, and nobody can sleep unless he does, except for prisoner 21, who is partially deaf (a former teacher who resisted the police and was hit several times with the butt of a gun).

Cell number 77. A small cell for 12 prisoners, currently occupied by 24 of us. Thick, high, concrete walls keep us away from the endless blue sky. One shared bathroom and shower. A small window. We watch the sky from behind the bars. Pictures of our family members are on our walls or attached to our locker doors. Three light bulbs, two are very dim, one is already dead. A rope spans across the room from east to west, for hanging clothes. With every sunrise, we wash our hope and hang it up on it, keeping it fresh until the night dries it, falling on us like a heavy quilt, dark clouds darkening our sky. Yet, stars penetrate the darkness and ignite our hope again, again, and again.

These walls of ours: twenty-one steps, north to south and eighteen steps, west to east. These walls here stand for more than what they may appear to be. They are the firsthand witnesses of our stories, tears, sorrows, and joys. Prisoner 9 keeps carving their section of wall, making a calendar. I have written a poem on mine, a poem by Nazım Hikmet. These walls, they are our most loyal friends. Who says they detain our freedom? Are we not free as long as our minds and spirits are? Have I not seen freedom in the bright green eyes of 13? Prisoner 13 doesn't care where he is, and it annoys me.

These walls of ours, they are meant to detain dangerous people. However, I can assure you, they deprive the outside world of the grace of these prisoners, like prisoner 13. Maybe these walls are meant to keep us safe—from the hypocrisy, lies, blood, and all that is unintelligible out there.

Through our small window, the sunbeams keep feeding our hope. It's what keeps us alive here. A sinner hopes to be forgiven, a mother hopes for something for her children, the poor hope to be rich, the rich hope to be richer, and when people don't have something to hope for they hope for their loved ones. Sometimes, we even just hope to have hope. And when we give up, we hope to die. We are as alive as our hope is.

Children give us hope, a reason to cling to life. But so much of what gives hope to people is considered a threat to the state, I guess. That is why they are imprisoned, why so many before us have been imprisoned. The Pharaoh of Egypt also tried to escape from what was prophesied by killing babies, thinking one of them to be the chosen one.

Yet, Moses came anyway—so did Jesus, and Muhammad, too (peace be upon them all). There is no escape for pharaohs. Some will be swallowed by endless seas wild as the waters of Dicle, and some will be hanged by their subjects.

Every day after breakfast, we are allowed to use a small yard. I never knew the sky was this far, this blue, this beautiful until I was deprived of it. I guess we only know the worth of what we have when we lose it. All the prisoners are outside today; even 13 seems happy.

Let me tell you more about my cellmates: there are eleven mothers, twelve babies, and me. Yes, Ayşe has twins. And yes, this prison looks like a kindergarten. I am a journalist, and other women are teachers, doctors, and housewives. As for the babies, I seriously don't know what to make of their stories. The eldest of them is eight months old. Ayşe sleeps with her twins on the ground on a thin mattress. They don't have proper conditions here for babies—though I suppose the real question is, how proper can a jail be for a baby? Our cells are cold. there is not much food, and there are no diapers. Out of desperation, what these mothers are going through is far beyond men's perception. It is true: women may be weaker physically, but mothers are mighty strong.

Most of these women's husbands are imprisoned too, at least since the so-called coup attempt. Their bank accounts have been confiscated, they've been fired from their jobs, thrown out of their homes, beaten in the streets, and tormented in the prisons. Take prisoner 4's husband, a twenty-nine-year-old teacher who was killed in prison. His mother found his dead body five days later, full of bruises and broken bones.

Prisoner 17 has something that she keeps in her pocket. She breathes from it, like an asthma patient using an inhaler. Some say it is a picture of her husband, G.A., who was tortured to death in a prison. Others say it is a pair of socks from her baby she lost two weeks ago. She still has her baby's cradle next to her bed. It's one of those classic wooden cradles, beautifully designed. And, whenever rocked, it makes a musical sound of reeds, triggering her tears. Guards make fun of her, call her mean names— "Miss scatterbrain who rocks an empty cradle," most of all. She is lost, that's for sure. But, after all she has been through, who wouldn't be? I still recall the night her baby was taken to the hospital. Her deafening shrieks echoed through the walls, piercing our hearts. The cruel world lay beyond. Her shrieks went on; the baby did not.

I want to write about the babies in this prison. Babies in prison... can there be any words stronger than these? Baby 13 was born here five months ago and was named Azad by his mother. It means freedom in Kurdish. His father has not yet seen him. As a matter of fact, nobody has seen his father since the day he was taken by police.

As for those who have put us behind these bars, I say unto them as Bediuzzaman said: "Do not just fear; tremble in horror." Fear would not decrease your greed, for you are drunk on power and are lost.

All the prisoners wear their numbers. Prisoner 13's birth certificate is addressed with the prison hospital. Prisoner 13 is happy, like all other babies are. Unaware of what has happened, what is happening, and what will happen to his family. His sweet world is his mother's arms. Everything about him, about his world, is beautiful, unlike what lies beyond these walls. I am jealous of him. In fact, I want to hate him. But I can't. Because I love kids. And do you know why I love kids? Because they remind me of how much we, as a society, have lost, how much we have given up by growing. So I whisper into his ears:

Azad, don't grow up boy, it is not worth it. And today when
he was crying in my arms, I whispered again (in Kurdish):

Azad

Xhem neke jè bonamın

Jè bona ku ez tucar baş nabım

Jè bona ku ez leşkerè roja reşım

Lè belè tu bèjemın

Azad

Heki ez hèsırè te ramusım

Eriti ya te è derbasèmın bıbe

Azad

Don't worry about me,

Because I will never be fine

I am a soldier of misfortune

But tell me

Azad

If I kiss your tears to enshrine

Will your innocence pass on to me?

2

Empty Cradle

Prisoner 17, who has lost her baby, is a former English teacher who was dismissed from her job after the staged coup. Her husband was already dismissed from his job, and their bank accounts were confiscated. A week later, one night, at the hours Satan reigned in the hearts of his fiends, police rammed down their door, handcuffed her husband, and took him away. The last time she saw her husband alive, he was being crushed under the tyrannical boots of paid dogs. Thirteen days later, his dead body, full of bruises and broken bones, was delivered to his mother.

The cause of death? A heart attack, officials wrote.

Prisoner 17 was already imprisoned when she heard

of her husband's death. She wasn't allowed to attend the funeral. The government didn't allow him to be buried in a known cemetery, either. Torturing him to death did not satisfy them; they wanted to continue tormenting him and his family by saying he was a terrorist and by burying him in the traitors' cemetery. The family was obliged to take his body to their hometown. Unfortunately, there too, the Imam assigned by the Religious Affairs Directorate refused to say funeral prayers. What was even worse was that so many of his friends were too afraid of the government to attend his funeral. So, he was buried. The bleak breeze of the factious, dark world went on, his pregnant wife in it.

Prisoner 17's psychological trauma caused her a preterm birth. She was taken to the hospital and she gave birth while handcuffed to a hospital bed. A new life was welcomed, to be caged by tyranny. Even though the doctors did not approve, officers took her to the cell, along with her baby, just a week later. But the baby was sick: 14 days later, one night we were woken up by a shriek like the "last trumpet" of the Doomsday. Prisoner 17 and the baby were taken to the hospital. Two days later, Prisoner 17 came back. Alone.

Prisoner 17 is not the only unfortunate mother in here. One afternoon, while I was lost in the pages of my book, I heard a scream. It was Prisoner 4, who has been here for the past three months with her daughter, Prisoner 51. She had seen news on TV, and she fell unconscious. A reporter mentioned a family whose boat capsized in the Maritsa River while escaping from Turkey to Europe. Hatice Akçabay, along with her three children, Ahmet Esat (one); Mesut (five); and Bekir Aras (seven); all four were found dead. We didn't need Prisoner 4 to tell us who they were: her cries did.

It was not the first time we saw people being carried away, killed in the waters of Turkey. Recently, this has become the unbearable new normal. Not long ago, the Maden family, a family of five, was found dead in the Aegean Sea while trying to escape Turkey for Greece.

Escape—from your own country! Being exposed to oppression in a country where justice is denied and judges are corrupt. I presume they had no other options. No one can blame them. When Moses ran from the Pharaoh, could anybody claim that it would have been better had Moses stayed and had his people killed? Besides, the

people who turned their back on Moses and said that he was indeed the righteous—but it was Pharaoh who fed them—should be the least of his concerns. Giving up on a cause in exchange for mundane gratifications is indeed a terrible trade to make.

I, too, sometimes escape from this prison, unnoticed. Since I am like a grandmother to Prisoner 13 (Azad), when I sing him to sleep, I sometimes put my head on his bosom and listen to his heartbeat. It's so peaceful, so beautiful—like enchanting music. Then, I inhale the scent of his hair by the lungful, and it takes me beyond. God, nothing on earth can have such a heavenly intoxicating scent, not even the rain.

And yet, still I am locked in a cell.

Cell number 77. A small cell for 12 prisoners, currently occupied by 24 of us. Thick, high, concrete walls keep us away from the endless blue sky. One shared bathroom and shower. A small window. We watch the sky from behind the bars. Prisoner 13 still doesn't care where he is, and it annoys me no longer. There are pictures of our family members on our walls or attached to our locker doors. We have three light bulbs, one already dead. A rope spanning from east to west for hanging our clothes on. With every sunset, we wash our dreams in the endless blue seas – of freedom, of life beyond – and hang them to keep them fresh until the sun's rays penetrate through our bars, drying them and shaking us to our harsh reality. Yet, the wind and birds flying free beyond ignite our hope again, again, and again.

Hope is a torch that's lit by faith. Hope is having faith in the victory of the light over darkness, even if that light is a shivering, fragile flame. In a life that is a graveyard of buried hopes, hoping is being optimistic in a moment of despair instead of being tormented by worries and pains. It's what you need the most. Within these walls, you die when your hope dies.

Notwithstanding, you still seek justice. You still seek humanity, or whatever is left of it. You still seek God with millions of desperate yet faithful eyes, which are banished or locked up in cells.

I must admit, at first, I was expecting to see thieves, assassins, and so on. However, I was shocked to see these many saints at the mosque, i.e. our cell.

As of those who have put us behind these bars, I say onto them; "Do not just fear; tremble in horror." Because soon you will prey on each other's carcasses, you will take a vow by offering up one another to your false gods. You are blessed and cursed at the same time by the very power that you wield. A sound will echo through the walls and prophesied your end. Being obliged to maintain this corrupt power is your curse, for you can't give up on it even though you are afraid. But the fear won't decrease your greed, for you are drunk on power, and you are lost.

As for those who have turned their backs on us, I say onto them; woe is you. What a bad trade it was. If what you seek is a peaceful world, then do the exact opposite of what politicians tell you to do. Because so many of them are factious fiends of Satan on Earth. But just like Pharaohs, soon, these politicians will be buried in the dusty pages of a cursed history. Then, we shall return to our lands. And you will hide behind walls of shame.

These walls of ours: twenty-one steps, south, eighteen steps east. These walls here stand for more than what they are. They are our worst enemies who have stood proud, witnessing our sob stories, tears, and sorrows by depriving us of all that we dream of at night as the darkness falls onto us like a heavy quilt. We carve them passionately as if enacting our vengeance. We carve dates on them, like a calendar. We carve faces on them, faces we miss, faces we hate. We carve poems on them; poems of hope, of life, of escape, of freedom, of fate, of misfortune, of everything that lays beyond, everything that they keep away from us. Wardens keep reminding us that it is forbidden to carve or to hang anything on the walls, and they charge us for the paint. Thus, this renewing and avenging circle goes on and on, more sharpened.

This concrete box I'm in is more like a coffin with headroom. It has been engineered with perfect precision. Someone designed this jail cell. Someone sat in an office, the sun shining on the window, and used their God-given talent to create something so soulless as to constitute additional punishment, as if taking our liberty did not satisfy them. Keeping us from those we love was not enough. So, someone didn't just build this cell, but poured pure hatred into its design.

Regardless of what the season is outside, it's always winter in here. The walls, the doors, the lights, and the window are all shrouded in white, are all cold as death. The reality of being caged begins to gnaw on you, body and soul, to break your spirit and your hope. Everything in here is iron and cold. The doors, the bunk beds, the food plates, the lockers, the windows, the bars, and even the wardens are of iron and cold as hell. Thus, the day you step in, as the heavy metal door is slammed behind, you begin to shiver and shrink, even in summer, like an early blossomed daffodil.

Knowing I will get no justice from judges who are bribed by corrupt politicians of tyranny, I pray to God to send a storm to knock down these walls. I pray constantly for this coffin to decay fast, but, deep in my heart, I know it is my body that's going faster.

It has been two years. But the snow has already occupied my temporalis and the mirrors no longer look kindly at me.

When you focus on time, the fall of one autumn leaf feels like it takes ages to kiss the earth.

In the first couple of weeks, you sleep a lot to waste time, to digest the harsh reality. The walls come for you, threatening to crush your bones at night. Fighting the idea of being caged makes you feel suffocated. You want to open wide the window and steal a deep breath from fresh freedom, a lungful, but the small window is blocked with bars. You plead darkness to leave you in peace with the solace of sunrise, but the night is still virgin. You pathetically learn that the hour hand cannot be trusted because it always comes late, like an old, lazy turtle. The decaying rusty minute hand of the clock begins to look like a wounded soldier pleading mercy from death, who has given up on fighting. And you give up on counting seconds when you realize that the beats under your left ribs are faster than the ticks of the old rusty clock on the wall. Thus, eventually, time loses its meaning. You only look forward to the sunrise. So, you accept your harsh reality.

In Kurdish we say;

Min sal diten danzde meh bun

Min roj diten danzde sala derbaz nebun

I saw twelve months lasting years

I saw days that lasted longer than twelve years

Every day after breakfast, we are allowed to use a small yard. I never knew the sky was this far, this blue, this beautiful until I was deprived of it. Blue is the color of freedom, the color of purity, like the innocence in the bright eyes of a child.

I think the notion of innocence references children because of their simplicity and their purity, which is unspoiled by mundane affairs. Such innocence is regarded as the promise of the world's renewal.

Unfortunately, these tiny bundles of innocence are being locked up behind bars. It makes me so angry at the world that I can bite the mountaintops. I guess such a renewal is no longer appreciated or welcomed.

We love kids because they remind us of how much we have lost, how much we have given up by growing, for the work of growing up in this cruel world. Growing up and seeing it was not worth losing that innocence, we repent gravely. So, it's a divine favor that God kept the true face of life from the children as they grow up, or else none of them would have had the heart to grow.

As for their mothers, none of them have wounds to be attended to. From head to toe, they are in pain. Therefore, these mothers have more faith in tears than they do in words. Particularly prisoner 17. I think it's against nature that a child should die before his parents.

I saw yesterday what Prisoner 17 keeps in her pocket. It's a pair of baby shoes. Within these walls, we all have something that keeps us connected to life, that feeds our hope. But in her case, all she has to adhere to is death. So, nobody ever wonders what she hopes for. All she has, all that feeds her hope, is a pair of baby shoes and a cradle.

Both empty...

3

Escape

I too sometimes escape from this prison, unnoticed. Sometimes with wind, sometimes with rain, sometimes with a cup of tea, and sometimes with these babies. I escape when I listen to Azad's heartbeat, when I inhale the scent of his hair by the lungful.

Normally, I look forward to the blue sky, during our time in the yard; but today, we are begrudged of that freedom, since the sky is covered with dark, sobbing clouds.

It's like a whispering in the air at first. There are still couplets of dead leaves fighting in the empty sky, carried through wires by the wind. Then, the splashes of the raindrops play drums on the concrete yard and the walls. The

more mesmerizing it is, the louder the music gets. A pet-richor perfume covers the air. I cover myself with a shawl and step into the yard with a cup of tea in my hand. The raindrops touch my face compassionately, like the lovely lit-tle fingers of a baby, soothing me. I close my eyes and take a deep breath, like it's my last. I believe I can hear the splashes of the wild waves whipping the shores of the sea beyond.

The rain is slower now, but it still falls. I fetch one more cup from the boiling tea. I lean over to the wall re-spectfully and as my hands engrave my cup, the steam of hot tea rises into the cold air from my cup, turning into my memories, my life. I escape with it, and it carries me beyond. I shut the world off, and let the steam dance and talk. Tea does that.

Tea carries memories and provides a feeling of warmth in a moment of shivering cold loneliness. Tea is a bond between you and your memories, between you and your loved ones. This bond is restored with every cup by its scent, its steam, and its warmth. Sometimes, a cup of tea may serve you better than a photo album.

Tea is life. Every cup resembles life, and resembles people who mingle for a short span in your life. You watch all the brewed leaves dive down harmoniously, one after the other, like whirling dervishes. Cherish its existence while it's hot, like life. Because, it tastes afflictive while it's cold, like death.

Tea calms the mind. The ripples in every cup are like the streams of life in my veins. Maybe tea is like the sun or the moon. It guides my mind to peace and purifies my soul. I am restored by its scent and its warmth.

Tea is peace. Tea is patience. Tea is digestions of indigestible truths – loss, sorrow, wrath, and all that we carry within, all that enslaves our souls. Leaf by leaf. You brew these leaves ceremoniously in a teapot, as if you are brewing your own life. The scent of brewed leaves calms your tumultuous seas by purifying your heart and mind with tranquil restoration. My grandfather used to prepare tea whenever he was angry or sad.

As my hands grow cold, like death, I see only dead leaves in my empty cup. I pay homage to the funeral of the dead leaves and stand up, dreary, as my escape is sabotaged by the death of my comrade.

I walked inside, smoking a poem into the breeze.

Someday,

When this storm is over,

When we anchor in a calm sea

We shall have tea

When sorrow, wrath, hatred and all that we carry

All that enslaves our souls and all that is not free

Of our unintelligible worries

Even our dearest memories

Shall brew in a teapot

And then, when they are no more sought

Next to a fountain, or under a tree

We shall have tea

4

The White Scarf

When they brought me in here, the sun was hitting the chest of the North Pole for the longest period of the year. My hair was darker than the reign of men on Earth. The trees, the grass, and the freshly planted saplings in my yard were still emerald green. Azad was not born yet, like many other babies in here – like many other babies beyond these walls. When they brought me here, the soil was still virgin.

Now, it has been so long, I have lost count of the days. Azad speaks now. I have witnessed babies crawling, walking, and talking in here, one stage after the other. My daughter told me that the saplings in my yard began bearing fruits this year. The colts have become stallions and mares and are now galloping freely. Seasons have changed through a second round, heading onto the third. The Earth has been shrouded twice in white. More than seven hundred times the sun rose and set, resentful of my skin. The Earth has finished its second journey around the sun, freely. It's all a matter of time, except for being a captive in a cell.

You have a lot of time in prison. But not much of it offers memories you will want to remember and cherish for the rest of your life. It does not offer much except for pain and sorrow, in contrast with the free world that is beyond your reach. A stirring world, containing all that you love and all of your loved ones in it. Your loved ones whom you grow together like the circles in the water, yet never meet.

Behind these walls, you miss a lot. Your kids and their heavenly smell. Your friends and drinking coffee with them. Going to a theatre for the latest movies. Listening to a new song. Watching the sea. The waves, the endless blue sky, and the colors of the spectrum in a rainbow, like the *Kesk, Sor, Zer* on the scarf of a beautiful Kurdish bride.

Walking in the rain – and not behind the wires or bars. Barefoot in the grass, and respectfully lying on it, watching the swift commotion of clouds fighting a battle in vain against compelling winds. Sleeping peacefully under an old tree and listening to the whispering leaves. And doing all of these whenever and wherever you want, without caring about time. That is freedom.

Like I said, I have lost count of the days. And I have lost count of my losses, like prisoner 27. On the news channel, the cause of death was stated to be pneumonia. But I knew her. She was brought here two months before. N. G. was her name, and she was my friend. She was imprisoned for teaching the Qur'an to children at an academy affiliated with the Movement that is being targeted by the government's witch hunt. She was touched by the icy fingers of pneumonia in here. As if her body was screaming allegiance to poverty, she became so thin that she could fit into my tears. Her health condition deteriorated last weekend, but she was told to wait until Monday to be taken to the hospital. She was taken on Monday, but it was too late. She was in a coma through ten sunsets, and then last night, I saw the news on the TV. She was gone. But her

empty bed kept moaning at nights for a long time, until a new prisoner was brought in.

Last week, they brought in a new prisoner, Prisoner 153. For three sunsets and three sunrises she cried, prayed, and recited the Qur'an in a quavering, slow voice, soothing like the whispers of the rain. When it rains, you don't look for reasons; it's just sad. So, we never asked her any questions regarding what her reasons were. Three days later, she was released. It was then I came to know of her tragic story in the newspaper.

Esra C. She and her husband had been teachers at a primary school. They were both thrown out of work after their names were blacklisted and then went into hiding with their baby. Her husband had cancer, but they couldn't go to the hospital for fear of arrest. The cancer consumed his body like flames consuming a candle wick. Eventually, as the pain became unbearable, she took her husband, Mehmet, to a hospital with someone else's ID card. Unfortunately, doctors told them that they were too late. Thus, neither surgery nor medications could make any change in his health condition. He left this world with a sunset revealing his true identity. At the funeral, the police handcuffed Esra and took her away, leaving her two-year-old baby orphaned in the world they had been running away from.

Not long ago, a similar tragedy happened in Ayvalık, Balıkesir. Two teachers, Hasan Aksoy and his wife, Sena Aksoy, were fired from their jobs and blacklisted. Trying to escape from Turkey to Europe in a boat, the boat capsized, and the waters swallowed Sena and her son along with five more lives: three babies and two women. The police handcuffed Hasan and took him away even before the bodies of his family were found. They sent him to prison without letting him attend the funeral.

The oppression and slaughter of the innocents by Herod and pharaohs are all solid evidence that the victims of these barbaric tyrants are indeed righteous in the way of God.

One of those victims, who unfortunately could not stand the oppression, was Prisoner X. She was brought in here seven months ago. Her baby, who is five months old now, was born in a nearby hospital while she was handcuffed to a bed. Two days before, late in the evening, she was taken away by the guards. About an hour later she was brought back – or rather, dragged like a piece of nothing. She collapsed on her bed next to her sleeping baby. Her face was pale like a snowflake. Prisoner 4 gave her a cup of water and asked something. But she didn't answer. She turned her face to the wall and pulled her knees toward her belly, shivering. The cold cell and bleak night were shrouded in a malevolent air. Everyone pleaded solace from sleeping. The half-death hunted down their weary eyes one by one; not even my snoring would bring them back to the light.

Later, not sure what part of the night it was, I was woken by a baby's cry: this had become a routine part of my life. Thinking his mother would take care of that, I didn't get up at first. But the baby kept crying. I checked the time; the night was still virgin. As I got up, somebody turned the lights on. The baby was still crying – and was his mother, who was acting weird. She was sitting on the bed and leaning her back tight against the wall, as if the cold concrete wall was the only thing she could trust in the world. She had her elbows wrapped around her knees pressed to her chest. Her hands covered her ears. She closed herself up like a hedgehog that felt threatened, instead of taking care of her baby.

While I was trying to calm the baby, prisoner 4 slowly touched Prisoner X on the shoulder, checking if she was alright. She suddenly shrunk herself away, screaming. Everyone was awake and scared now. Other babies were woken up and started crying, too. Prisoner 4 pointed at the crying baby, saying she needed to breastfeed him, but she pushed the baby away. Why was she acting like this? She looked like she didn't want the baby near her, but it pained her. I could see this in her eyes. It was as if she felt guilty, as if she was blaming herself for a shameful act. None of that made sense to me. She has been bizarre since last night they brought her back. Did they give her a bad news that could be worse than her current situation? Did they do something to her? I heard in Erdemli, a biology teacher was taken into custody with her daughter, and police threatened to rape her daughter if she wouldn't comply. Did they do something similar?

The babies were back to sleep about an hour later, as were some of the mothers. I didn't sleep that night. Prisoner 4 fell asleep, leaning over Prisoner X's bunk bed, holding her hands. With the help of medications, Prisoner 4 finally fell asleep, too. Throughout the rest of

the night, she kept talking in her sleep. She kept pushing away something or someone, though I could not see
what; she kept waking up screaming; she kept crying
over and over and over again until the darkness could
not endure her ordeal, could not cover her trauma, and
yielded to the sun.

Yesterday, early in the morning, the guards came to
count prisoners. The moment they came in, she began
screaming. But they didn't care. Even seeing her screaming and pulling her hair like the insane, they laughed with
sheer insolence, and they taunted her with sheer impu-
dence. And, in the evening, when they came to count prisoners again, which is a daily routine in the prisons, I was
obliged to watch the same devastating scene. Later, I gave
her some painkillers, and she slept. Last night was a ca-
tastrophe, and everybody was tired. We all fell one by one,
like weary ancient knights. Later that night, when I woke
up for morning prayer (*fajr*), I went to take ablution, and
I saw her body – hanging from the high window bars by
her white headscarf.

I informed the guards, and they came with the police officers. The guards didn't seem surprised. The police

didn't untie the scarf from her bruised neck, but cut it in half with a knife. We heard her body fall. Later, as the police were carrying her cold body out, one of them took the scarf off her black-and-blue neck and threw it back into the cell. She was finally free.

For years, this country has treated the bearers of the headscarf like outcasts, and recently, they have started killing the bearers of the scarf with it.

Since they brought me in here, the sun rays hit the chest of the North Pole two times for the longest period of the year, resentful of my skin. My gray hair is now as sacred as a white scarf that covers a devout soul during prostration, and is paler than the skin of a prisoner who has lost a life in captivity.

Like prisoner X, she was finally free.

5

My Mother's Rugs

After tilting at windmills for two months like Don Quixote, I decided to spend my time on things that would help me digest my reality before it digested me.

More than two years before, when I learned that some prisoners were working in jobs like farming, drawing, knitting, wood carving, and many other fields for making money and spending time on something useful, I talked with the warden of the prison and donated my mother's loom on condition that I alone would use it until I am free.

I joined the rug knitting club. On Monday, Tuesday, and Wednesday, from nine to twelve, prisoners worked in the company of guards. Thus, I started working in a work-

room. After two hours of lessons, I was allowed to free work for one hour more. This is when I knitted my life, motif by motif, into the rugs.

I knitted Satan and his fiends. I knitted a corrupt system. I knitted a corrupt society. I knitted corrupt politicians. I knitted corrupt judges. None of them will know that it's their own story. I knitted angels. I knitted prisoner 17's empty cradle and a pair of unworn baby shoes in her palm. I knitted Ayşe and her twins sleeping on a thin mattress on the ground. I knitted Azad's birth certificate. I knitted Prisoner 153 crying in prostration. I knitted her standing next to a dead man's body on a bed. Nobody will know that he was her husband. I knitted Prisoner 27's thin, sick body that could fit into my tears. Nobody will know that she was my friend. I knitted Prisoner X's body hung to the high window bars by her white scarf. I knitted her black-and-blue neck and her white scarf. Nobody will ever know what they did to her. I knitted a woman being raped in the prison. I knitted the woman handcuffed at the funeral. I knitted the women giving birth while being handcuffed to hospital beds. I knitted babies behind bars. I knitted the Maden family next to a capsized boat.

I knitted drowned bodies and deflated life vests. I knitted fearful eyes on Turkish shores. I knitted hopeful eyes on the boats. I knitted tearful eyes on European shores. I knitted boats heading to dreams. I knitted my teacup. I knitted my losses. I knitted my tears. I knitted my fears. I knitted my dreams. I knitted all I had. I knitted all I could reach. I knitted all I couldn't reach. I knitted all I missed. I knitted my daughter. Overall, I knitted a life in captivity. But nobody will truly ever know for what special art form they are or what they mean. Nobody but me. An art form that I learned from my mother.

My mother knitted rugs. She was an artist. She used to teach young girls the art of knitting and embroidery. When we were kids, she embroidered lovely trees, flowers, and nightingales. Even she though she denied it, we knew the nightingale was not the only bird she knew how to embroider. My father had a beautiful voice. Years after my father was killed, she started knitting again. But this time she started embroidering dark figures, wild animals, owls, and shrubs, all looking formidable – like the guards of this prison. Circles into circles, windows into windows, and doors into doors, all getting smaller and smaller until your hypnotized eyes led you into a puzzled, dark nothingness. The ornamental one that hung on the wall of our sitting room was emotionally overwhelming. Although she said it should remind us of my brother Ceco staining her favorite rug with tomato paste, we knew its red was blood. Besides, her favorite rug was ornamenting her bedroom wall with the figure of an angel – sunny smile and eyes full of light, so bright they could save any soul lost in the shadows. The angel was rising from a cemetery full of faceless stones, but both wings were chopped and lying on his gravestone. One night, thinking we were asleep, I remember her saying, "How joyous you look, how ardently you are smiling against life. Because the 'You' on the wall does not know 'You' are dead yet." She had a huge collection of rugs. But she refused to sell them, even when we couldn't pay the bills. Years later, not sure whether it was time or inflicted pain that hit her harder, her eyes repented to the colors and went dark.

Everyone and everything goes eventually. Death is just an excuse. Missing my father so dearly, my mother welcomed her excuse wholeheartedly. Or, maybe cancer did.

After my mother passed, the weaving loom was taken to the garage and hung on the wall, like most of the rugs woven on it. Darkness wove over the sun. Snow wove over the earth. The earth wove its way around the sun. Days over days, seasons over seasons, and lives over lives were woven lustfully, cheerfully, artfully, but nothing over the weaving loom.

I drove in and out every day from that garage and saw the loom hung up on the wall, untouched. The decaying rusty nails on the loom began to look like deserted dogs barking at heaven. The scattered strings on it looked more anile than the river Dicle. The wooden parts, completely covered in dust, looked more ancient than any bone left in the soil. So, in time, it became like a ghost of unappreciated art – like every prisoner in this cell, invisible to the world.

The art of handicraft rugs couldn't weave a way out against the rapid development of textile. Those produced by the latter were cheaper, like the judges of this corrupt system. Thus, people bought it, used it, but never respected it, never called it art. Never ascribed any meaning or never felt any emotion looking at it. Because art carries emotion, art requires devotion, art carries meaning, and art carries memories of its artist. Like my mother's rugs and her tears. Yes, tears are the most sacred form of art, the most honest manifestation of emotions.

Art is imitation, the reflection of truth, of reality. On a canvas with a talented painter's masterful strokes; on a mouth reciting poems enchantingly; on a paper where each word shouts thoughts and confessions that ears are deaf to; on a rug from the long and beautiful fingers of a damsel, each thread carrying emotions and reality, like a life in the prison, all in an artistic form.

Art is rare, and rarity is beautiful, like my mother's rugs.

6

Pain Has No Side

Since my childhood, I have always admired the perseverance of my leftist friends for resistance. As a young Kurd (whose kin have been slaughtered repeatedly, our culture and history plundered, our language forbidden and existence denied), every time I heard or witnessed oppression and massacres perpetrated by the abusive power of governments or of its authorities, I wanted to stand against it like them. Fight against it like them.

However, later, as my friends started targeting me with their antagonistic stereotypical socialist jargons (which some of them didn't understand themselves), by holding my faith responsible for all those crimes and all

the death and destruction in the Middle East, I resented it.

On the other hand, to my conservative friends, my leftist friends were a bunch of faithless defeatists. Yet I knew in my bones, it was my leftist friends, referred to as faithless defeatists, who mostly have stood with the oppressed regardless of their ethnicity and faith. I realized people do not welcome those who are not one of them, or those who do not think like them. Thus, eventually, I wiped out all those fusty intolerances with the back of my right hand and kept my faith under my left rib. I shaped my life, not with such intolerant ideologies and antagonistic doctrines that yielded nothing but death and destruction to its bearers, but with righteous norms that I felt were at the very center of my existence. I am neither a leftist, nor a rightist. I side with no one. I have only one side: my left side. And it beats beside the innocent and the oppressed as long as it beats. Because the pain hurts the same.

7

Why I Write

All I have been through and all I have seen, have made me who I now am: an imprisoned journalist, a writer.

Kurdish singer Ahmet Kaya once said,

"There isn't a manly man who will live in Turkey without getting into trouble."

Not that I intentionally write to get into trouble. But I write the shrieks of the oppressed against injustice imposed by the hands of tyranny – the same hands that exploit the power of this beautiful country. I write the screams that don't reach the conscience of the authorities. I write because pain hurts the same. I write because I am sad. I write because I am angry. I write because that's all I have.

I write about things I want to forget. I write about pain I can't forget. I write for the grace of these children. I write because I am not free. I write because I feel free. I write because that's all that will be left of me.

Writing.

Fighting against injustice of this wretched, filthy, and cruel world to create a peaceful one, where everyone is free and equal, has been my passion. And I have been carrying a fire in my heart to fulfill this passion.

This passion is like a vigorous love, ever burning and everlasting. It drags me like fire drags a moth. It has an overwhelming power. Sadi Shirazi says, "If you fly to love, it will burn your wings." For Rumi, "If you don't fly to love, what is the point of having wings?" I know this passion will put me in trouble. I will probably end up burning my wings. But, what if that's the whole point of life?

Being born in the land of fire and blood, I have been through ordeals not many people would have survived, and writing is my way of honoring this struggle, a way of honoring the fallen and a way of igniting hope. You can't write unless you are hurt. And, when you're wounded, let it bleed. Let it bleed because writing is healing. Writing is relieving. Writing is when you are most honest. Writing is all you are.

Writing is bleeding on paper, word by word, though the wounds can't be seen, can't be touched, and can't be heard, but can't be unfelt, deeply. Writing is protesting across sentences. Writing is swearing, spitting against injustice, against things that you don't approve, yet you don't have the power to change.

Writing is protesting against the government for the destruction of Kurdish cities. Writing is a way of honoring the freedom the pen provides.

Writing is singing for Ali Ismail, who was beaten to death by police officers. *He must have suffered a lot*, mourned his mother.

Writing is pawing a stone for Berkin Elvan. A fifteen-year-old kid who was sent to the market for bread. He never returned. He was killed with a police officer's gas cartridge.

Writing is remembering the fallen, like Taybet Ana. For seven days, her body was kept in the street of Silopi by the savages, the lost souls who have gone astray. Trying to

take her body away, her husband was shot and her brother was killed. The wildlings that have killed were thrilled, yet not satisfied, and pined for more blood to be spilled. And for seven days, her children guarded her body against wildlings, not knowing that no creature could ever be as wild as those who have killed their mother, and for ages have been killing their mothers, fathers, and siblings. A mother was killed, by the direst damned subjects of God, who said they were trying to bring heaven to the world. A mother was killed, by those who said that heaven was under the feet of mothers.

A mother was killed, and no one ever knew what she had been through, how she lived. But her death had a sound that echoed beyond for others like her. Because rape, torture, massacre, assimilation – these have been their faith, and now the wildlings are promising more. The destruction of their cities and homes, killing, the burning of children, are being rejoiced, celebrated in the country of Rumi, Mevlana.

A mother was killed. Her name was Taybet Ana.

Like the Kurdish politician Selahattin Demirtaş (he, too, is currently imprisoned) said:

"They were not killed by the country. They were killed because they didn't have a country."

I write because I don't want to see one more son lost, one more mother suffering from such a loss. I write because I can't be silent like a grave. I write because the innocent and oppressed need a voice. I write because pain has no language, pain needs no language. I write because tears fall the same in every language.

Love is the best verse God has ever revealed on Earth, and hearts are temples. Despite all this hatred, pain, and suffering, there echoes a prophecy on the walls of my temple, saying that there is still hope. And this is a cause worth fighting for, worth writing for.

Now you tell me: am I getting my wings burnt for a wrong cause?

8

Loss

Şiirlere nakşettiğim, meğer koskoca bir yalanmışsın

Varlığın umut olur ama, kavuşmadıkça ısıtmazsın

Uğruna ne canlar yitirdim ey kör olası özgürlük

Ne çok dışlandım, katledildim, oysa kaderimdi Kürtlük

It was the beginning of spring, still the doldrums of the year: as the mountains and hills remained shrouded in white. Nature was yet a virgin, quiet and bashful. But the wind had already begun to warm, prophesying spring. The trees that were naked and brittle were going to grow over the span of a few moonless nights. The sunrays piercing the heart of the shrouded mountains and hills were going to hit limbs pointing the red bud of the new life stirring at the tips of the crackly brown bark. Soon, the snowdrops were going to make their appearance, not letting white disappear on the skirts as snow jilted. Even though the high mountains of Kurdistan mostly remain blanketed in white, like a damsel's scarf, year round, as the sun pierces their chests, the snow melts layer by layer, enlivening the hectic life in the valleys and providing water to their inhabitants. Soon, the hills behind Texchan were going to blossom, and within a few sunsets, Texchan village was going to be the prettiest place on Earth. The newborn lambs and goats were going to jump joyfully around their mothers, appreciating life, while shepherds mounting the hills after them worked off their wintery rust.

Like the plants and animals, the children of Texchan sensed the coming of the sun and were going to greet it wholeheartedly by joining the joy of spring. Soon, the snow melt was going to unblock the roads to the city, and peddlers were going to bring the balls, toys, popsicles, and ice cream the children were so looking forward to. Children were going to chase after the ice cream man. Mothers were going to cook fresh vegetables after having dried stocks throughout winter, and fathers were going to buy fruits if they could. People were going to breathe in the smell of soil, touch it, cultivate it, and appreciate its fertility. After all, they all knew it's what they came from, and it's what they were going to return to.

Yet that fertile soil was not just prophesying spring, but so much more to come that would change the valley's residents' lives forever. Everything was in harmony; everything, until they showed up.

On a chilly morning, they came. They rammed our doors and stormed into our houses. They searched the houses, breaking our things while their dogs barked. They gathered men of age in the center of the village and handcuffed them backward. They bent them on their knees. Some of these men, like my uncle, resisted and got hit with the butt of their rifles. And they took them away. They took my father away. Thus, Texchan village was no longer the prettiest place on Earth.

For two months, we anxiously waited in fear, but my father didn't return. The snow melted, and the village was stuck. Mud flowed from the hills and mountains. The first blossoms were hit by an unexpected frost, and

the red buds of the new season shrank in their brown cradles. Some of the trees remained naked, and with wind blowing, they looked like deserted dogs barking at heaven. It rained a lot, as if nature was trying to purify the Earth of sins. Thus, I didn't go out much. There was nothing out there that I cared to see. I didn't see children running after the ice cream man. Maybe he didn't come at all. The peddler did come, but he didn't stop in our neighborhood. Who cared: his toys were stupid and cheap. My father's hand-carved dolls, cradles, and toys were always my favorite ones. On the first day of my school life, before sending me to school, he gifted me with a wooden pen. It was elegantly hand-crafted from wood and had the phrase *Jın, Jiyan, Azadi* (Woman, Life, Freedom) written on it. I knew he made it for me with his own hands. I still keep it, and with it, I write my life.

Accused of helping enemies of the state, two months later, my father and his friends – one of them limping – appeared at the court in bruises. They were found innocent and released. However, on their way home, my father was kidnapped by people driving a "white Toros." They said they were working for the state and forcibly took away my father, as his friends reported.

The "white Toros" was a locally produced Renault, which was not only popular for its durability in the countryside, but also known to be used by JİTEM (gendarme intelligence and counter-terrorism) at that time, and their appearance was regarded as a bad omen. One would better be dead than be in that car. People rarely returned to their families once taken by them. And those who did come back were never the same. Even though JİTEM's existence was denied for years by its Headquarters and the General Staff, in Kurdish regions every man and woman was familiar with their loathsomeness, assassinations, and drug dealings. People of Turkey's Kurdish regions were used to seeing them dressed like guerillas, or sometimes like civil folks, casuals. They could dress like anyone and do anything they wanted. No laws applied to them; they *were* the law.

That year, in autumn, they also took my uncle, S.H., who was the elected mayor of the town under the banner of the Kurdish political party, HADEP. He disappeared for a long time and when he came back, he was not the same. He could barely walk, eat, or sleep for a long time. He was tortured so much that his injuries later caused him to be partially paralyzed. That's what I meant when I said one would better be dead than be taken by them.

After my father was taken, things were never the same. My mother stopped weaving rugs, and she cried whenever she was alone. Thus, I tried to keep her company as much as I could. During the day, when relatives and neighbors visited, us kids were sent out, so we wouldn't hear their scary assumptions – as if anything could be scarier than being an orphan. Their visits were meant to show empathy, but they only left my mother in tears.

During the night, thinking we were asleep, she cried while watching the roads.

Days flowed like the waters of the Dicle River, but even water hurts if it flows through a wound. Those flowing days took our hope; no good news was seen on the horizon.

Hopelessness consumed my mother. She became so thin that her finger couldn't hold her wedding ring. She was listening a lot but was not hearing much. Her heart was not ready to digest what people were telling her. She didn't have that strength. None of us did. She was barely eating. Her grief was affecting my baby brother, too, and he was crying all the time: she could not breastfeed him enough. If she would ever fall asleep, exhausted from tears, she would wake up screaming. In short, after my father was taken, life was like death, but nobody had died.

Yet.

For two months, we waited. But no news came. Meanwhile, my mother visited police stations over and over again, carrying us with her. But there was no record of my father being taken again. They said they released him among others, and they could not be held responsible for what had happened to him afterward. Initially, they pretended to be concerned by making phone calls and saying we were welcome to check everywhere we could. But we knew their efforts wouldn't change anything. They asked if we had enemies or knew of honor killings. Later on, as our visits yielded no benefit, they made it obvious that they were being disturbed by our visits. They started making fun of my mother. But my mother was not a spiritless woman. She insulted them back, and they threw us out in the end. Finally, they said they were going to put us in jail if we ever came back and disturbed them again. My mother was not afraid of them for herself, but for us, she stayed away. If she was put in jail, what would become of us children? She strictly taught me how to get back to the village with my baby brother and younger sister if ever such a thing happened. She tried to reach people who had power. But they all were getting stuck, saying something beyond their power was going on. Every door we knocked on for help, was shut back on our faces. And every time we returned, empty-handed, the face of Texchan village was changing.

I was praying to God to send a storm to knock the walls of wherever my father was kept (as neighbors speculated). I prayed constantly for the corrupt system to decay fast, but, deep down in my heart, I knew it was my mother that was going faster.

***

Watching the endless empty roads through windows became part of my mother's life. She wanted to believe that he would return to us someday. And, like a quivering flame of a candle, she wanted to light the way back to us. Like a lighthouse. But father was not lost at sea. He wasn't lost to anything natural. Rather, he was lost to a kind of Gog and Magog.

Life, fertility, peace, compassion, mercy, and so many similar virtues are attributed to mothers. That's why we have *mother* earth, *mother* language, *mother*land, *mother* soil. But, unfortunately, after we lost my father, my mother also lost her life and her peace. She became like a desert as our neighbors gossiped. They blamed her for not taking care of us well. But we knew it was not true. They didn't leave us in peace. So, one day, mother came home, saying she had rented a place in the city, and we had to move. There was not much for us in the village anymore. Besides, coming to the city every week twice or thrice for father was not easy for her, as she dragged us after her. We didn't take all we had, because she said, soon, we were going to move back – once father returned. So, we loaded father's van with essentials, and left Texchan at sunrise. I knew even then: the summer morning would remain in my memories the rest of my life. The village was still silent, like a grave. I could hear the waters hitting the stones in Axur creek. Leaves were fighting a battle with the wind on the branches of the trees that lined the creek. The fresh dewy grasses were bowing allegiance to the wild wind. I could feel the wind on my face and my damp eyes. The roads were still empty when the sun rose. My mother started the engine and left our narrow street, getting on the main road towards the city. In the neighborhood, a barking dog started chasing us. Mother killed the barking with the accelerator. The village disappeared as we took to the dusty roads.

***

Going to police stations two or three times every week, we came to know that there were thousands of others lost like my father. We heard people fearfully whispering such stories, but we didn't know someone personally who had lost a family member. I was old enough to know that Kurdish names were forbidden. That's why most of us had two names: one for our lives and one for the state. Listening to Kurdish music was also forbidden – that's why our music cassettes were always kept hidden. Patients were thrown out of hospitals for not being able to speak in Turkish. Students, some of whom were my friends, were constantly slapped or punished by teachers for not being able to speak Turkish. Not that they were trying to annoy the teachers, but the only Turkish they knew, they learned from TV.

The stories went: family members were disappearing, and people who were going after them faced the same fate. Whenever someone was trying to rise against injustice and oppression by becoming a voice of the innocent and the oppressed, he or she was disappeared or somehow silenced. And there was not a single competent or judicial authority willing to change the misfortune of these people. It was then that I promised myself to grow up leading a life for this cause. Standing against injustice with the oppressed, regardless of their dissimilarities. It was then that I promised to be their voice. After I lost my father.

***

After we moved to the city, my mother was leaving me at home to take care of my siblings. She was meeting with others to look for father. Every day, she was leaving home after I was returning from school, and she came back with the dark. A few months later, mother went back to the village and brought her weaving loom. She started knitting again. But this time, she started embroidering dark figures, wild animals, owls, and shrubs, all looking formidable. Circles into circles, windows into windows, and doors into doors – all were getting smaller and smaller, until your hypnotized eyes were led into a puzzled, dark nothingness. When we needed the money, she also started accepting orders and knitted rugs for people. I was also helping her, and we started making enough money to pay for lawyers and others who were helping us. She did have a huge collection of special rugs. But she refused to sell them, even when we couldn't pay the bills. I knew they were important to her. They were her memories. Her memories with my father that she wove knot by knot into the rugs.

Darkness wove over the sun. Snow wove over the earth. The Earth wove its way around the sun. Days over days, seasons over seasons, and lives over lives were woven lustfully, cheerfully, artfully, but nothing different was woven over our lives. My mother stopped going to police stations and started to meet with other people who had also lost their family members. Not a day went by without a new missing case of a father or a son gone, their whereabouts whispered in tones of fear in dark corners.

Years passed, but nothing changed. Those left behind started working with associations that stood for human rights. There appeared a group of mothers, known as *Saturday Mothers*.

Years passed. I am not sure whether it was time or its inflicted pain that hit my mother harder; her eyes repented to the colors and went dark. We gave up on finding father alive; we just wanted his dead body to be delivered.

Have any of you lost a father? I did. And even now, at the age of 41, every time I see a father and a daughter walking hand in hand, I feel that pain branded under my left rib. I never found him. I never had his body to bury, to have a proper funeral. I never got to say prayers, to read the Qur'an beside his body, to cry and mourn after him, to know where he lay, to visit his grave on Holy Eids.

Everything that I couldn't do became part of my life. It's why my mother's tears and elegies never stopped until she passed away. Day and night don't make any difference; being an orphan always has the same dull color. There is no such thing as forgetting the pain: I just got used to it, and I learned to live with it. It's like death, but I still breathe.

9

Freedom

When I woke up for the morning prayer, the darkness was abandoning the Earth. A heavy smell of orphanhood, from the children, slunk over the cell's walls. I prayed, and then I prepared some tea. Sobbing clouds covered the sky, and it was chilly. Though the high walls of the prison blocked the sight of sunrise on the horizon, I could still see the light in the yard. Dead leaves were fighting the empty sky, carried through the wires and into our concrete yard by the wind. It started slow, like whisperings in the air at first, and then the splashes of the raindrops started whipping the concrete yard and the walls like a merciless chariot rider.

An enrapturing petrichor perfume started covering the air. I stepped into the yard with a shawl covering my back and a cup of tea in my hand. I shuttled across the yard several times, watching the sky beyond the tall concrete walls. I hated the walls. I could feel the raindrops touching my face, like the lovely little paws of my cat Berfo, silken soft and soothing. I closed my eyes and took a deep breath, like it was my last. I could hear the splashes of the wild waves whipping the shores far beyond.

I fetched one more cup of boiling tea. I leaned respectfully over to the north wall, and as my hands engraved my cup, the steam of hot tea rose into the cold air. The rain stopped. I crossed the wet yard several more times, thinking about my testimony for the trial where I would appear that afternoon. If I would be released, the thought of leaving these babies behind made me shiver. I felt desperate.

After lunch, I appeared at the trial. There were a few friends, a few journalists, and my daughter. I repeated the same things: I didn't murder anybody. I didn't commit any crime. I didn't break any law or cause violence. But, I did address some questions most people were afraid to ask. Questions that I had the right to ask as a journalist. Questions I had the right to know as a citizen from whose taxes their salaries were given. Questions that were whispered by the public in fear. Questions such as how could a parliamentarian become a millionaire in such a short time on a state salary? Questions about corrupt ministers and parliamentarians. Questions about nepotism. Questions about imprisoned elected parliamentarians of the opposition parties—elected representatives imprisoned just because they were not afraid to stand against the injustice of this government. Questions about journalists who were imprisoned just for asking brave questions or revealing the government's crimes. Questions about speculative deaths. Questions about mothers and babies who were imprisoned without any proof of crime while the law stated that, even if proven to be otherwise, a mother with a child could not be imprisoned until the child is of a certain age. Questions about students who were imprisoned just for being anti-government or protesting against its actions. Questions about the government affecting the decisions of the courts. Questions about the government controlling the media. Questions about government methods that violated the law. Questions about freedom

of speech and human rights. Questions about what this beautiful country has become in the hands of its politicians. Questions, questions, questions.

My questions were no different than before, and the judges knew that I was innocent, but I believe that the decision was sent from above. There was too much pressure on the public, and they needed to breathe for one round. Thus, the judges set me free. But I still had to go to the police station every week to sign papers, to prove that I would be staying at the same address. Because I was not allowed to leave the city, and I could not travel abroad.

Some so-called journalists from the "pool media," paid dogs of the government, and a few of my friends were waiting outside for me. They were called "pool media" after certain corporates were made to contribute hundreds of millions of dollars to a "pool" to purchase one of the largest media organizations to provide positive coverage of the media in return for highly profitable public contracts. My friends waited on the other side of the road so as not to get bitten. One of the so-called journalists asked if I was ashamed to be on the side of traitors, terrorists. See, this is what the world has become. People who could not bear seeing the fall of a star from the sky so it might get hurt were called terrorists. I didn't expect any different from them: they were doing what they were hired to do. Demonizing whoever the government targeted and praising whoever they were told to. It was only a matter of obedience for them to lapidate an innocent resisting voice. Who cared if their target was innocent, once the government pointed at them? Dogs do that once their owners take the collar off.

I didn't waste a single word. I knew it didn't matter, as the headlines of the pool press would be sent from above: "The Traitor Journalist Is Released." And they were, with similar headlines appearing in 19 different newspapers.

I went back to prison to get my belongings in the company of a few soldiers. My cell mates were so happy for me, but it was killing me that I could not feel the same thing for them. Because I knew, this corrupt system was not going to release them any time soon. However, they all knew that I would be struggling for them to be released. It was so hard to leave them behind. After I hugged them all and said goodbye, right before leaving the cell, prisoner 13 held on to my leg in tears, not letting me go. His tightened face bit his shivering lower lip; his dewy green eyes struck my heart. I hugged him, breathing in the heavenly smell of his hair, and kissed him several more times. His tears fell on my neck like soft morning rain. His mother pulled him back, which made him cry even louder. I left the cell and the heavy clunky metal door rammed behind me. I could still hear him crying. As I mounted up the stairs, his shrieks in my heart I bore, long after I could hear him no more.

I went home, cleaned and dressed up, and threw myself out on the streets. I missed walking in the open streets without facing the walls. I hated the walls. After dinner, we went to the Kadıköy coast. I took a few cups of tea watching the sea. I loved the sea blending in with the sky. I loved it not being blocked by the tall walls. I walked on the coast until my legs were heavy. I walked back to my previous tea house and took a few more cups of tea with lemon. It was chilly and my daughter was asleep in the car. Poor child: she didn't even ask to go home. But it was not as cold as the tall cell walls that I hated. I leaned back on the ottoman couch, watching the sky and the sea, until darkness widowed the earth. It was a marvelous thing to see the sunrise without being blocked by the walls.

I hated the walls.

Next morning, I woke my daughter and we went to a place where the famous Van breakfast was served, Van Kahvaltı. I had missed this breakfast a lot. We ate the renowned *otlu peynir*, a slightly crumbly, potent cheese spiked with an herb called *sirmo*, along with *nan-e tandure* (bread), and so much more. We ate accompanied by the Kurdish musician (Dengbej) Shakiro's velvet voice. The music tasted different outside, compared with how it was felt behind the walls.

God, I hated the walls.

We went home to get some sleep. But an hour before sunset, I was back in the same spot, watching. It was Saturday. The streets were full of people. The guy who brought me tea said that my photos were in all the newspapers and news channels, and in none of them anything good was written or said. That explained the reason why some people were giving me mean looks. I told him that it was fine with me, since I didn't have to please the whole society. And as a journalist who knew the media quite well, I told him to be careful what he believed and what he didn't believe. Besides, in a land where oppression was on the rise, only someone who lacked a spine could offer the olive branch to everyone, particularly to some politicians, the avowed servants of Satan. He nodded his head in affirmation and said that he was a dedicated teacher until two years back, when they fired him from his job in a school based on some made up pieces of evidence provided from the "pool" newspapers. He whispered a quote by Malcolm X, "If you're not careful, the newspapers will have you hating the people who are being oppressed and loving the people who are doing the oppressing," and he went to the young couple sitting on the farther table, with a broken smile on his face. Against all the scandals that were going on, one only needed the bravery of a child to scream that the emperor had no clothes. But nobody did. They only stood by and watched the filth, the oppression going on unconscientiously like the cold concrete cell walls.

And I hated the walls.

***

I watched the sun turn red and then fade beyond the horizon like the color on the callused palms of a weary

worker. I watched the boats and the seagulls fight the trou-
bled sea until my friends came, and then we went to have
dinner. In the restaurant, two young guys approached me
and with foul language accused me of being a spy of for-
eign countries.

They accused me of being a traitor because the people
I stood up for were mostly affiliated with *Hizmet hareketi*,
who, for them, were the enemies of the state. I tried to ex-
plain that I was standing with them not only because I was
one of them, but also because I knew they were innocent,
they were oppressed. With their thousands of schools and
universities built and operated around the world, Hizmet
(literally "service") has been advocating for universal ac-
cess to education and its members have shown that they
have nothing to do with violence or all those crimes the
government has been blaming them with. They were not
supporting the corrupt and cruel government, and this
has made them the main target of a sweeping purge that
has been underway for the last few years.

Moreover, in a democratic state, people have rights,
and their rights are protected by the constitution of that
state. The laws of the state are to be applied to everybody

equally. In their case, if there was a proof of a committed crime or their involvement with violence or a so-called coup, as the government claimed, then the judiciary authority could manifest the evidence to the court, and only the court could deal with it, impartially. No one should be tortured to death in the prisons. No one, let alone a mother with a baby, should be imprisoned just because he or she doesn't like the government.

But they didn't want to hear me. They were getting louder, and other people were disturbed. My friends pulled my arms and dragged me out. The security just stood by and watched the whole time, lifeless as the cell walls.

***

The next day, I faced a similar situation at the shopping mall. The owner of the store said that traitors were not welcome in his store.

The day after that, my daughter came home early from her new school in tears. I went back to the school furiously. I learned that her classmates had said something bad about me, and she fought with them. What was even worse, I heard some students' parents wanted my daughter expelled from the school because they didn't want their children to be exposed to treacherous ideas from her, and that the treachery was in our family traits. The thing is, there isn't a child born a chauvinist or a racist. They get exposed to such contagious diseases from their parents.

When the water rises, the fish eats the ant. When the water recedes, the ant eats the fish. This is the way of nature. Just because they held the seal, it does not mean he who held the seal is the real Solomon. It just means that the water had receded.

The day after that, my daughter didn't go to school. She wanted to go back to her previous boarding school. It was two and a half hours' drive from home. It was so hard leaving her again – it made spending three years behind the cell walls seem easy. And, God, I hated the walls.

After I came back, I went directly to the coast. I rented a small boat and rode up the Bosphorus Sea as if avenging all the pains that tore through my chest. I carried freedom deep in my lungs and rode along the sky. The allegiance of the clouds lay with me as I tore through the dark blue cascades, as if challenging all the misfortunes that were awaiting me. I rode as if sworn to catch the horizon, as if repentant of living with people, as if sworn to leave all the wicked hearts behind. I rode to eternity.

Being born in Mesopotamia is like being left barefoot on broken glass. You bleed if you walk, and you still bleed if you don't. I chose walking. For two months, I faced similar hatred from different people over and over again. I saw the rancid face and blindness of a corrupt society. I saw the hatred that had swallowed the whole of society. I saw people calumniate their relatives and neighbors to the government, and after they were imprisoned had confiscated their property. I saw people treated like outcasts just because the government put them on a target. I saw people breathing in air, but breathing out hatred. I saw people carrying water to the mill with buckets in vain. I saw people striving to plaster the sun in vain. I saw a society that was torn apart into a zillion groups by the hands of mischievous politicians.

I had read that once people made idols from halvah to worship and then ate them when they grew hungry. Now, the halvah was superseded by money and power. But the people are still the same greedy ones. I saw the government control the media and punish every resisting voice;

I was constantly bothered for standing with those few resisting voices. I knew brothers who killed each other for the power of the state that they worshipped, and the people who tolerated this violence were imprisoning mothers and newborn babies. I saw politicians, disguised under religion, accumulate interest from a politically religious society. I saw a religious government imprisoning people and then confiscating their property. I saw people believe that all of the injustice and oppression that they had witnessed at the hands of their government to be for the good of the state they worshiped.

I saw people cutting all of the colored flowers in gardens except the green ones. I saw a tree in the garden with so many different birds singing their own songs, but the farmer only wanted to hear the crows so he shot all of the other birds, including the nightingales. I saw people whose grandfathers' names were Ares, Adad, Igor, and whose grandmothers were Vivian, Asie, and Idil but claimed to be Turkish; and I saw them barking at other ethnicities, saying that they did not belong to this country. I saw them say, "either love it or leave it." I saw the racist, chauvinistic people who had lost all of their human traits;

they are walking corpses. I saw people who proudly kept the record of lives they ended. And they are now teaching it as history to coming generations, hoping they will follow their footsteps. What good could they possibly have to contribute to the coming generations, to the world, other than death and destruction?

I saw a family with two beautiful children. The mother's name was Cennet, and the father's name was Devlet. They had two equally beautiful and distinctive sons. The first son's name was Agit, and he was from Cennet's first marriage, which is why his stepfather never loved him. The second son's name was Hakan, and he was privileged by the father. The mistreatment from his stepfather became the main cause of Agit's hatred towards his step brother. And Hakan's hatred towards his brother was because he learned it from his father. The only thing they had in common was their love for their mother, Cennet. I saw that beautiful family destroyed just because of their father's hatred. I cried.

I saw a religion, not the one that God revealed, but the one the government made, and I saw that the worshipers of the state were more than the worshipers of God. It reminded me what Caliph Omar (RA) once said: "If you do not live as you believe, you start to believe as you live." I saw scholars who had sold their faith in exchange for the money and power provided by the government. I saw people who believed that just because they had religion, they didn't need morals.

I saw people who were seeking intellectualism and wisdom in wine. I saw millions of people who had no knowledge, but had millions of ideas about everything. I saw people who believed in everything they heard without investigating its truth. I saw a society which thought they knew everything. Yet, their supposedly omniscient knowledge was nothing but the contamination of social media.

The people that I saw were hateful because they didn't want to see or hear what they had become. But I was nothing but a mirror they wanted to shatter, nothing but the sound of their conscience. They will have to kill me to not see or hear me. But without me, they will become conscienceless devils.

I saw mountains getting lost behind the hatred and injustice. I saw humanity sinking and the bells ringing for it.

I wondered when the sun would rise from the west, when the stars would fall on us like rain and the earth would bear no more. But then I saw a child. A child was painting the sky in blue, and I saw hope again in those shades of blue.

10

Departing a Suffering Land

My lawyer arrived last Friday morning, fearful for my safety. He told me that two of my journalist friends who were set free right after me were taken into custody again that night. They also imprisoned the judges who had set them free. Not long before my trial, the President himself targeted us directly by publicly saying that even if people like us were found innocent and released by courts, "his people" would deal with us. The government was intentionally provoking people against each other. People were already threatening me in the streets; and behind the prison's bars, we were threatened with hanging or torture. The government has already killed many "prisoners" by torturing them to death. Only God knows how many are still lost.

I could not bear the risk of being imprisoned again. Cold, crowded cells, cruel guards, terrible food, iron bars, and tall concrete walls. God, I hated the walls. No, I could not take that again. My friends in Europe had been sending invitations to me since the day I was released. But there was something they didn't know. They didn't know that I was not allowed to leave the city, let alone leave the country. But I would rather die than be imprisoned again for crimes I had not committed. One of my friends reminded me of people who smuggled Syrian refugees to Europe for money.

The smugglers. As a journalist, I wrote about them several times. But I never thought I would someday desperately need one. Under normal circumstances, neither would my friends come up with such a suggestion, nor would I consider it a good idea. However, circumstances were far from normal. Those smugglers, the ones that were always talked about? There were not easy to find. I went to Küçükçekmece, Bağcılar, Sultangazi, Fatih, and Esenyurt. Those were the districts with the most Syrian refugees. I

spoke Kurdish most of the time, to make an intimate con-
nection with the locals, since many of them were Kurds of
Rojava. I left my phone number with some people in the
tea houses (*çayhane*), and requested that they reach out
to me if someone helping refugees were found. Saturday
evening, someone called me from an unknown number.
A thick male voice, speaking in Kurdish, asked me to go
to the Bağcılar center, Kardeşler tea house to meet him at
11:30 pm.

I went there alone. The tea house was so crowded,
noisy, and humid that as I walked in, I could feel the mois-
ture clinging to my clothes. It felt thick as I breathed it
in, and it coated the inside of my throat. Heavy cigarette
smoke that smelled sharp, like the burning of timber, filled
the air. People were gathered around tables playing games.
The thin clattering sound of rummy tiles dominated the
sounds of other games at other tables. The waiter, masterfully holding seven empty cups in his left hand, came towards me with a smile on his face. He put the pen he was
holding on his right hand behind his ear and shook my
hand with his emptied right hand. With a cigarette burning between his lips, he told me that I was expected in

there, showing me the clunky iron back door. I hated iron doors. I looked at the door he was pointing at: there was no handle on it. I noticed a rope swinging from a small hole in the place of where the handle was supposed to be. I pulled the rope and the clunky door opened, groaning.

At the table, under a dim light, there sat a slim guy, with a cigarette burning between his twig-like fingers; a young fat guy sat next to him. I stepped in and the iron door closed, groaning again. I sat on the chair I was shown, and we talked about how the process would go. The slim guy was the older one, and in charge. He did not ask my name, and he did not answer my question about who he was. He said it did not matter. I asked for a guarantee, about how I would be sure that they would take me to Europe. Because they were asking for a lot of money. Eighteen thousand Euros. He laughed. He said they were not thieves. He said they were doing it to help desperate people like me, and they were not conscienceless smugglers. The guy was funny. But I had seen funnier ones. The world most certainly had. The dictators praising republicanism and democracy. The corrupt parliamentarians preaching honesty and decency. The so-called religious people worshiping the state, money, and power, while giving sermons about worshiping God. The paid dogs of a dictator claiming to be the judges of the nation for justice. I had seen more shameless disgusting clowns than this puny, conscientious smuggler. Anyways, there was no other option. So, I accepted his terms. He told me to be in Balıkesir four days later with the money. I went back home and started packing up.

The next morning, I had breakfast with my brother and my sister, and I told them everything about my plans. We spent the day together. I strictly cautioned my brother to take care of my daughter until the end of the semester. I didn't want to change her school again. I strictly cautioned them not to call me as well from their mobile phones; because, in several cases, when the government could not round up people they were looking for they arrested their family members instead. Who cared if they were innocent, and who said the people they were looking for were not?

I got dinner with a few of my journalist and writer friends. They were afraid of being imprisoned – or even worse. The situation in the country was not going to get better any time soon, and it worried them. Some of my friends had already moved abroad because they were not feeling safe, even though they were not against the government. In fact, most of them were not even interested in politics at all. But to this government, one was either with them or against them.

I personally didn't like politics and most politicians, and I have always made that notion clear. I believe they provoke anger and hatred; they polarize people and divide the whole society. They are like ticks, feeding on dissimilarities and societal wounds. Unfortunately, in an unjust society, these politicians became famous. And, in such a society, education and educated people are cast out, because they hold a mirror to reality.

I made a phone call to the prison and talked with prisoner 13 and his mother. Prisoner 13 said he had missed me and asked me when I would be back in there. Prisoner 13's mother encouraged me about the steps I took regarding leaving the country, which I discreetly told her about, and she prayed for my safe journey. She also said she prayed for me after hearing about the article I wrote for a European newspaper regarding what people have been going through in the prisons.

Before leaving Istanbul, I went to the police station again and made my weekly appearance. I tried to not look suspicious, but my heart was like a wild horse galloping across the Mediterranean grasslands. I quickly signed the papers I had to and left on my tip toes, trying to look calm; I don't even know if I breathed. Being afraid of the forces that were supposed to keep us secure was the most disgusting shame on the account of this country.

I was not allowed to leave the city and thus had to avoid the main roads. It made my journey longer, but at least it was safer. Besides, I got to see the beauty of the countryside.

On the way to Balıkesir, before leaving Istanbul, I went to see my daughter. I wanted to spend one day with her. I told her everything about my plans (apart from the smugglers) and promised that I would take her too once the academic year was over. Besides, she didn't have to take this dangerous road with me, since she could travel with her passport.

I went to Balıkesir and met the funny smuggler. He was accompanied by a scary-looking young guy whose face, arms, and shoulders were masterfully tattooed. His left shoulder was fully covered with the head of a dire wolf, and on his arm it was written, "winter is coming."

His right shoulder was fully covered by a three-headed dragon, and on his arm, it was written, "I will take what is mine." On his right hand it was written, "dracarys." On his throat it was written, "valar morghulis." I was pretty sure that he had more of those tattoos on his body. He looked disturbed and even angry as I studied his tattoos. I gave the funny smuggler his money, and the tattooed guy took me into a black Volkswagen Transporter. The windows were tinted with black film, and I could not see where we were going. But from the swinging of the car, I understood that we were not traveling on regular roads. About two or two and half hours later, the car stopped. The tattooed guy appeared at the door, saying that we had reached our destination, and he pulled me out. There was a small wooden cottage, and he told me that we were near the seaside, so we would wait in that wooden cottage until the night was at its darkest hour. We walked to the cottage; he opened the wooden door and almost pushed me in.

The cottage was full of people waiting desperately to go to somewhere they heard was better. I counted twenty-one pairs of desperate eyes. There was a thin kid amongst them, probably as old as my daughter, an eleven or twelve-year-old girl with emerald green eyes. I came to know that her name was Rojda. She was with a family that spoke Kurdish with an Amed accent. She had a deep, meaningful look on her face that made her appear sophisticated. And with those emerald green eyes, she gazed deep into my soul, as if she could read my mind, my memories. Her hair was of the color of fallen leaves, browned and silken with the initial autumn rains. But she looked weary, almost sick, with that Mesopotamian sand skin. And those green eyes seemed in pain, praying for mercy. I have always trusted eyes more than I have trusted words. As for the others in the cottage, some of them were speaking in Arabic, some of them were speaking in Kurdish, and a family was speaking in Turkish. The shocking thing was that only nine of them were from Syria. All the others were from Turkey.

In Mesopotamia, we say if pain had a language, it certainly would be Kurdish. No one has suffered as much as the Kurds have. We are the Orphan Nation. But everyone in the country has suffered at the hands of this state. Not only us Kurds have faced injustice.

The girl and her mother slid over and I sat down next to them.

11

The Silver Lady

My mother slid over for her to sit with us. It was late afternoon. We were all waiting in the wooden cottage near the seaside when she showed up at the door. Another guy in tattoos was standing behind her and pushed her inside. The wooden door was closed again.

A tall slender lady, presumably in her mid-forties, stood in the middle of the cottage. Her gray-white hair was like waves of cotton clouds on pure sky, elegantly reflecting the light of the setting sun; each strand moved freely in the sea-born breeze, as a compliment to her dignified stature. With her silver hair, she looked like a heroine my father used to tell me about in one of his stories.

She carried a red leather bag that went perfectly with her red shoes and the red shawl she was wearing around her neck. Her honey-colored eyes studied every one of us, a smile on her face. My parents and both of the Turkish speaking families greeted her. She looked familiar to me, but I didn't remember meeting her. We all were new there, and everyone had a worried look on their faces, except her. She looked back at me with a smile and gazed deep into my soul, as if she could read my mind. I couldn't take my eyes away from her, as if I was hypnotized, until my mother slid over, giving her a space to sit. The woman nodded her head appreciatively and sat down. She exchanged a couple of words with my parents. Father told her that he liked her writings. Later on, she closed her eyes for a while, as if thinking. Then, she took out a notebook and a pen from her red leather bag and started writing something. Her pen was exquisitely handcrafted from wood and *Jın, Ji-yan, Azadi* (Woman, Life, Freedom) was written on it. She wrote nonstop for almost an hour, without caring about a cottage full of people staring at her admiringly, as if this time, she was the one hypnotized.

Well after midnight, when the darkness was so dense

that you could not find your nose and so menacing that a knight would not dare go out to pee, we were told to get ready to leave. Without making any noise we left the wooden cottage, one after the other, and went after the rude guy with tattoos. We walked in haste for about fifteen to twenty minutes through dark roads and olive gardens until we reached the sea. A boat was waiting for us there. But I didn't think it was big enough for twenty-four of us. The lady with gray-white hair and red bag started arguing with the tattooed guy. The silver lady said she wasn't told that it would be a small speed boat, and she said they were endangering the lives of innocents by misusing their desperation. The tattooed guy and the captain were getting furious and pushed us towards the small boat. But the silver lady looked so pissed off: she said that they didn't keep their promises, despite all the money they took from her. The captain raised his voice and said to everybody that they were more than welcome to go back if they wanted, and their money would be paid back. I was sure he knew that nobody would. At that moment, everyone was drowned in silence. They looked at their family members, and bowed their heads in desperation. My father looked at

my mother, kissed me on my forehead, and hand in hand, we moved towards the small boat. There was a Turkish family with a swaddled baby, and the mother was crying. Nine people amongst us were from Syria, where waters ran red and tasted *like death*, where fire smelled of screaming flesh *and death*, where songs were only sung of war *and death*, and they didn't have any choice except for running *from death*. Thus, even though I didn't think they completely knew what sort of evil we Turkish citizens were running from, they all knew that no one would put his child in a boat unless the water was safer than the land.

The silver lady was the last person who got on the boat. But as soon as she got on, this time she asked for a life jacket, and the captain looked even angrier then before. I thought they would throw her off the boat. I don't think it was her intent, but I really liked that she was annoying them; they were rude to us, particularly the tattooed guy, who was always scolding people, yelling at and pushing them. The tattooed guy went in and brought one life vest, throwing it towards her, with anger blazing in his eyes. This time, she asked them to give life jackets to everyone in the boat. The captain looked at her, yelling that they had no time to lose and they had enough jackets for everybody if needed. But, he said, if he was kept busy with trivial worries while he should be piloting the boat towards Greece, we might be late or even be caught by the Turkish coast guard patrols. Hearing about Turkish coast guard patrols from the captain, everyone fell mute. The captain told everybody to be patient and without any trouble, we would (inshAllah) reach Greece in less than two hours. Everyone held onto their family members and the captain steered the boat into the unknown darkness.

Finally, we were on our way to the new lives we had dreamed of. I was excited. The sea was wavy. The weather was cold, and the wind and splashes of water cut like sharp knives into our faces. I saw that one of the Turkish-speaking mothers was trying to protect her baby from the cold weather and splashing water. With every wave, the boat was sinking more into the waters. Overloaded with twenty-four of us, the boat, which had only six leather seats, was already down by the stern.

About thirty or forty minutes later, I heard a scream from the woman on the bow of the boat. Yes, the stern was fully in the water. Then, everybody started screaming in panic. The captain nonchalantly told us to be patient and not to panic. He said, as boat was still working and on the move, this was normal. The silver lady told him to give life jackets to everybody as a precaution, but unfortunately, the captain said the only jacket they had was the one she was wearing. We were shocked. We were wet. We were scared. We were cold. Eventually, the captain stopped the engine, and while coming towards us, involuntarily, he said, "We are going to sink." Everybody started screaming in panic, and holding onto each other. The captain looked like he didn't know what to do, either. Along with my father and three other men, he tried to empty the water out of the boat. I used my shoes to help them. But, unfortunately, it was of no use. The waves were so powerful. The captain went back to restart the engine. But, it didn't work. And not long after that, with a big wave, half of the boat went deep down in the waters, and half of it was standing upright on the surface. We all tried to hold on to the portion of the boat that was still on the surface of the water. Everyone was crying and screaming desperately. One of the Syrian refugees, with his broken Turkish language skills that he probably learned in camps, told everybody to

call 158 Turkish coast guard patrols, 156 gendarme forces, even 911. But the silver lady yelled at him not to call
them. The same bleak fear was on the faces of all Turkish
citizens as those forces were mentioned, and at that time,
I could see that the Syrian refugees didn't understand why
we were so afraid. But the lives of their families, their children were at risk. So, those who had phones tried to reach
them, despite the fear they had on their faces – all except
for the silver lady.

After several tries, finally, the coast guard answered
one of the Turkish speaking guys, as we all were screaming for help. They asked him to send them our location.
With one hand holding the portion of the boat that was
still on the surface of the water, he sent them our location with the other hand. The captain and the tattooed
guy were nowhere to be seen. Then the upright portion of
the boat also started to sink; soon, it completely vanished
into the dark waters. We had nothing left to hold on to –
nothing but hope.

Everybody was screaming for help. The waves that
were lapping up the boat hitherto scattered every one of
us. Mothers were separated from their babies and their

husbands. It was like the doomsday stories my father used to read to me. The last time I saw the Turkish speaking man. He was trying desperately to reach his wife and his baby, who were taken away by the wild waves. I saw the silver lady desperately trying to reach an Arabian family for help, but the waves were so strong and before she reached them, they vanished in the dark blue. I saw the family that was from Rojava, and they vanished, too. Then I saw the second Turkish speaking family desperately trying to swim together with their son, and I saw the silver lady swimming towards them. She made it. She reached them, and I saw her shouldering their son. Together, they swam towards us. My father was a swimmer. He told me and my mother to hold on to him. Once others reached us, my father told them that we needed to swim together. Screaming for help and struggling to stay alive for so long, everybody was exhausted. The sea was cold. The weather was cold. And the darkness was menacing.

I don't know how long we swam, but it felt like ages. The Turkish guy was holding his son's foot, and his son's hands were clinging around the silver lady's neck. The man sank. Then he appeared again, breathless. He looked

at his wife and his son in desperation for one last time and he disappeared, this time for good. Soon after him, his wife's hand slipped off her son's tiny foot, and she, too, disappeared into the dark waters. After a couple of minutes, their dead bodies were on the surface of the water around us. The wild waves mercilessly dragged them like the fall wind drags dead leaves. Their son remained clinging to the silver lady's neck. She was crying, quietly. We swam, swam and swam. I heard my father saying, "I am tired." I heard him saying to my mother, "Please forgive me." Then, my mother pulled me off his neck in tears, and not long after that, he disappeared. My mother was also exhausted. We all were, but we kept moving our legs to stay on the surface of the water. The silver lady was trying to encourage us, saying that help was on the way. I don't know how much time passed, but my father's dead body was still following us on the water. I still remember my mother looking at me for the last time. Then, she pushed me towards the silver lady, and she disappeared into the dark.

We were in the middle of nowhere. The dead bodies of my parents were following us on the surface of the water. The silver lady was trying her best to keep us both on the water. But the life jacket was not enough to support all three of us at the same time. The other child had no power to even cry. It was freezing cold and the boy had lost his voice. The silver lady was desperately struggling to succeed. But after we swallowed the salty waters that burnt our lungs, she should have realized that we wouldn't make it together. So, she removed the life jacket, and she put the jacket on me. She harnessed the life jacket around my body and put the Turkish kid on my shoulder. She told me not to worry, that the jacket could easily carry both of us because we were not that heavy. She tried to swim with us for a while. The help was still nowhere to be seen. Maybe they did come but couldn't find us, since the wild waves were dragging us. I could see that she could no longer keep up. She told me to find her Greek friend whose address was written on the last page of her notebook, if someone from Greece saved us. And she told me to find her daughter, if someone from Turkey saved us. She said her daughter's school address was written behind her photo in the notebook. The notebook was in the pocket of the life jacket she put on me. She tried so hard for a little more. Then, a huge wave hit us, and she disappeared in the dark waters.

The night was no longer dark. My parent's bodies were gone. It was so cold that I didn't know if I had any other feelings except heartache, and I was in so much pain that I didn't know what part of it was for their loss. I saw the silver lady's dead body re-appearing on the surface of the water. Even the silver lady's death had a beautiful color: impartially dull, yet noble, like her stature. Or maybe it was just because I admired her selflessness, her struggle for others. Who can tell? But I can tell that we were all on our own in the middle of the sea. Two orphan children were dragged into unknown waters by the waves. The boy no longer had enough energy even to hold on to me and I no longer could feel my legs. I had no strength left. I wanted to let the waters take me to wherever they took my parents. But the silver lady entrusted me with this kid, and I had to remain faithful to her trust. I had to honor her struggle and her sacrifice. I remembered how she struggled to save people when she could've only worried about herself. She saved this boy, and after my parents were gone, she saved me. So, I had

to stay alive and keep this boy alive until someone came to help.

I don't know for how long we were dragged by the waves, but I no longer had the strength to even scream for help when I saw the boat that was coming towards us. I only waved with one hand while the other one held the kid on my shoulders. When it got closer, I saw that it was a coast guard patrol's boat. Two of them, with their uniforms on, jumped in the water and helped us to get in. Finally, we got out of the water. Probably one of the guards was asking questions, because his lips and hands were moving. But I could not hear anything. I closed my eyes.

When I opened my eyes again, I was on the arms of one of the guards who saved us, and he was getting off the boat. I don't remember what the people were saying. I don't remember what I was feeling, apart from the freezing cold. But only one thing is still clear: a guard was running towards me in tears with a blanket in his hands, and a female guard, again in tears, was holding the Turkish kid tight onto her bosom to keep him warm. And I felt the warmth of compassion, the warmth of mercy. I felt peaceful.

I don't know how many days passed, but when I opened my eyes again, I was in a hospital, surrounded by nurses. A middle aged uncle came to the room all in whites, probably a doctor, and the nurses started talking with him in a language I didn't understand. This is when I learned that I was not in Turkey.

They brought an interpreter, and asked me if I was feeling good. They asked me if I could tell the police officers what had happened. So, starting from the moment we left our city until we were saved by the guards, I told them everything I remembered. One of the police officers was taking notes, and the other one was asking questions. When I came to the part where the sea, like an unfathomable black hole, started swallowing people – including my family – I saw pearls falling from the police officer's cheeks, getting his note page wet. The other police officer, who hitherto was interrupting me from time to time with his questions about things he wanted to know more about, cleared his throat like he had a question, but failed to ask, as if the words were knotted in his throat. He gave up.

We were taken under protection. We were safe now. We were supposed to be sent to a place where asylum seekers were kept, but the silver lady's Greek friend, whose address was written behind the photo she gave me, came for us and took us both with him. The police officers must have informed him after I gave them his address. We are living with him now and we are safe.

Dear Shilan,

Your mother has written her life story in her notebook (the notebook was in the pocket of the life jacket with which she saved us). It covers the events up until leaving the wooden cottage, where I saw her for the first time. But that's not where her life ended. The girl with emerald green eyes she saw in the cottage was me. My name is Rojda, and I owe her my life. I thought I needed to complete her life story as the firsthand witness of her sacrifice. So, I wrote everything that happened until we were saved in her notebook, and I am sending you this notebook. Your mother was everything a girl like me would want to be. She was a fighter. She was an angel. She was a poet, just like she wrote in one of her poems I found in her notebook. The poet of fallen angels:

I have fought gloriously, and I lost
After all, it's only matter of life and death,
isn't life the biggest cost
Glory isn't only in winning;
it's hidden in the cause for which you've fought
Epics have been written, but nothing on us
Yet I lived, suffered, cried, bled, fought
And I lost like most of us
I am glorious for I am the song of life,
in the name of fallen angels
I am the poet of lost battles